THUMBELINE

Hans Christian Andersen
Illustrated by Lisbeth Zwerger

**Newly translated from the Danish
by Richard and Clara Winston**

William Morrow and Company/New York/1980

Printed in the United States of America.
1 2 3 4 5 6 7 8 9 10

Library of Congress Cataloging in Publication Data

Andersen, Hans Christian, 1805-1875
   Thumbeline.
Translation of Tommelise.
Summary: The adventures of a tiny girl no bigger than a thumb
and her many animal friends.
[1. Fairy tales] I. Winston, Richard. II. Zwerger, Lisbeth. III. Title
PZ8.A542Th   1980   839.8'136   [E]   80-13012
ISBN 0-688-22235-8   ISBN 0-688-32235-2 (lib. bdg.)

THUMBELINE

Once upon a time there was a woman who dearly wanted to have a little tiny child of her own, but she had no idea where one was to be had. So she went to an old witch and said to her, "I so dearly want to have a little child. Won't you please tell me where I can get one?"

"Why, I think we can manage that," the witch said. "Here is a grain of barley. But this is not the kind that grows in a farmer's field or the kind that is fed to chickens. Plant it in a flowerpot, and you will see something special."

"Thank you very much," the woman said, and she gave the witch twelve silver pennies. Then she went home and planted the grain of barley. Almost at once a large, beautiful flower sprang up. It looked much like a tulip, but the petals remained tightly closed as if it were still a bud.

"What a pretty flower!" the woman said, and she kissed the lovely red-and-yellow petals. But the moment she kissed it, the flower gave a loud *Crack!* and opened. Now you could see that it really was a tulip. And there, seated upon the green heart of the flower, was a tiny little girl, as dainty as could be. Since she was no bigger than a thumb, she was called Thumbeline.

An elegantly varnished walnut shell served as her cradle. Her mattress was made of blue violet petals, and her comforter was a rose petal. There she slept at night, but by day she played on the table, where the woman placed a basin ringed by flowers whose stems rested in the water. A big tulip petal floated on the water, and Thumbeline would sit on this and row herself from one side of the basin to the other. She had two white horse-hairs for oars. What a sight that was! She could also sing, and no one had ever heard so fine and sweet a voice.

One night, while Thumbeline lay in her pretty bed, a hideous toad came hopping in through a broken pane of the window. The big, wet, ugly toad hopped right down on the table where Thumbeline lay asleep under the red rose petal.

"She would make a fine wife for my son," the toad said, and she took hold of the walnut shell in which Thumbeline was sleeping and hopped away with it, out through the broken windowpane, and down into the garden.

A broad stream flowed through the garden. The ground around it was boggy and muddy. Here the toad lived with her son. Ugh, he was just as ugly as his mother. And when he saw the pretty little girl in the walnut shell, all he could say was, "Jug-a-rumm, jug-a-rumm."

"Don't bellow so or you'll wake her up," the old toad said. "She might run away from us, for she is as light as swansdown. We'll put her out in the stream on one of the lily pads. That's as good as an island for her, since she's so light and small. She won't be able to escape, and in the meantime we can fix up our parlor down under the mud, for that is where I mean us to live."

A great many lilies grew in the stream, their flat green leaves floating on the surface. The lily pad that was farthest out was also the largest. The old toad swam out to it and placed the walnut shell, with Thumbeline inside, on it.

The poor little creature awoke very early in the morning, and when she saw where she was she began to cry bitterly, for there was water on all sides of the big green leaf and no way at all for her to reach land.

Meanwhile, the old toad sat deep in the mud painting her parlor the yellow of marsh marigolds, which she applied with a reed brush. She meant to have a place her new daughter-in-law could be proud of. Then she swam out with her ugly son to the lily pad where Thumbeline stood, for she wanted to fetch the dainty bed and set it in the bridal chamber before bringing Thumbeline there. The old mother toad bowed low in the water and said, "May I introduce you to my son. He is to be your husband, and you will live in a lovely house in the mud."

"Jug-a-rumm! Jug-a-rumm!" was all her son could say for himself.

They took the little cradle and swam away with it, while Thumbeline sat all alone on the green lily pad and wept, for she did not want to live with the ugly toad or have her ugly son for a husband.

The little fish that swam in the stream saw the toad and heard what she said. They stuck up their heads to have a look at the tiny girl, and they found her so lovely that they thought it a shame for her to go down into the mud to live with the toads. That must never be. So they gathered together in the water around the green stalk of the lily pad, and they nibbled away at the stem with their teeth. And long before the toads could return, the lily pad broke loose and floated away down the stream along with Thumbeline.

Thumbeline sailed past many places. The birds that sat in the bushes saw her and twittered, "What a pretty little girl." Her lily pad floated farther and farther, so that Thumbeline traveled far beyond the borders of the country.

A white butterfly kept her company, flying round and round her and at last alighting on the lily pad, for it was entranced with little Thumbeline. And Thumbeline herself felt happy, for now the toad could not catch her and the countryside they were sailing through was lovely at the moment, with the sun shining on the water so that it looked like gleaming gold. She took off her sash and tied one end around the butterfly, and the other end she attached firmly to the lily pad. So the lily pad skimmed along faster and faster, carrying Thumbeline down the stream.

Suddenly a big June bug came flying by. He caught sight of Thumbeline and instantly locked his claws around her slender waist and flew up into a tree with her. Meanwhile, the green lily pad floated down the river and the butterfly flew along, for it was fastened to the lily pad and could not get free.

How frightened poor Thumbeline was when the June bug whisked her up into the tree. She was most concerned about the white butterfly she had tied to the lily pad. There it perched now, and if it could not break loose it would starve to death. But the June bug gave no thought to that. He settled down with her on the biggest green leaf in the tree, gave her the nectar of flowers to eat, and paid her compliments, telling her how pretty she was even though she hardly looked like a June bug. Then all the other June bugs who lived in the tree came to pay a visit. They looked Thumbeline over, and the Miss June bugs fluttered their feelers and remarked, "Why, she has no more than two legs, the poor wretch." "And she has no feelers at all!" they said. "And what a smell her body has. Ugh! She looks like a human being." All the June bugs agreed that Thumbeline was the ugliest thing they had ever seen. And yet the June bug that had captured her still thought she was pretty. But since all the others said she was ugly, he at last believed them and no longer wanted to have her. She was free to go wherever she pleased, he said. He flew down from the tree with Thumbeline and deposited her on a daisy. There she wept because she was so ugly that the June bugs despised her, and yet she was the loveliest little creature imaginable, as delicate as the finest rose petal.

All summer long poor Thumbeline lived alone in the great woods. She wove herself a hammock out of dried grass and hung it under a big dock leaf so it was protected from rain. She gathered the nectar of flowers for food and drank the dewdrops that hung on the leaves every morning. So the summer went, and the fall, but now winter was coming, the long, cold winter. All the birds that had sung so sweetly for her had gone their ways. The big dock leaf she had lived under shriveled into nothing but a yellow stalk; she herself was so small and delicate that it was only a matter of time before she would freeze to death. It began to snow, and each snowflake that fell on her was like a whole shovelful flung at us, for the snowflake was big and she was the size of a thumb. She wrapped herself up in a dry leaf, but it did not warm her; she shivered with cold.

Close by the woods where she was living was a large grainfield. But the grain had been harvested long ago. Only the dry, barren stubble still stood above the frozen soil. The stubble made a whole woods for her to walk in, and, oh, how she shivered with cold. She came to the entrance of a field mouse's burrow, a little hole under the stubble. There the field mouse lived safe and sound; she had whole rooms piled high with grain, and a sweet-smelling kitchen and pantry. Poor little Thumbeline waited outside the door like any poor beggar maid and begged for a barleycorn, for she had had not a morsel to eat for two days.

"You poor little thing," the field mouse said, for she was a kindly old soul, "come into my warm house and eat with me."

She promptly took a liking to Thumbeline and said, "You're welcome to stay with me through the winter, but you must keep my house clean and tell me stories, for I do like to hear them." And Thumbeline did as the good field mouse asked and found life very cozy down in the burrow.

"We will soon be having company," the field mouse told her. "My neighbor usually pays me a weekly visit. He has an even finer house than mine, with many big rooms, and goes about in a coat of handsome black velvet. If only you could get him for a husband, you would be very well off. But he happens to be blind and won't be able to see you. You will have to tell him the finest stories you know."

But Thumbeline had no wish to please their neighbor, nor to have him for a husband, for he was a mole. He came and paid his visit in his black-velvet coat. He was rich and well-educated, too, the field mouse said. His home was more than twenty times bigger than the field mouse's, and he certainly had a lot to say on all kinds of matters; but he could not tolerate the sun or pretty flowers. He spoke of them with contempt, for he had never seen them.

Thumbeline had to sing for him, and the mole fell in love with her because of her beautiful voice. Yet he said nothing, for he was inclined to keep his feelings to himself.

He had recently dug a long tunnel from his house to theirs, and he invited the field mouse and Thumbeline to stroll in it whenever they liked. However he told them not to be afraid of the dead bird that lay in the tunnel. It was a whole bird that still had its beak and its feathers and must have died quite recently, since the winter began. It happened to be lying just where he had built his tunnel.

The mole took a sliver of rotting wood in his mouth, for that gives a faint glow in the darkness, and led the way, lighting up the long, dark tunnel. When they came to the place where the dead bird lay, the mole used his broad nose to dig away at the earth and made a big hole in the ceiling so the light could come through. There in the tunnel lay a dead swallow with his pretty wings folded close to his sides, his legs and head also drawn in under his feathers. The poor bird was surely dead of cold. Thumbeline felt so sorry for him, for she dearly loved the birds. All summer long they had sung and chirped so sweetly for her. But the mole kicked the swallow with his short legs and said, "Now that's an end to his piping. What a misery it must be to be born a bird. God be praised that none of my children will be like that. A bird has nothing but its chirping and must starve to death in winter."

"Ah yes, a sensible person like yourself may well say so," the field mouse agreed. "When winter comes, what do the birds have out of all their chirping? They are bound to starve and freeze. And what a monstrous size it is, too."

Thumbeline said nothing, but when the two others had turned their backs, she bent over the bird, stroked the feathers of his head, and kissed one of the closed eyes. This might be the one who sang so sweetly for me during the summer, she thought, the one who gave me so much pleasure, the dear, pretty bird.

The mole now closed up the hole he had just dug and escorted the ladies home. But that night Thumbeline could not sleep. She got out of bed and went and found some hay in one of the field mouse's storerooms. She also found some soft cotton there. All this she carried down the tunnel to where the dead bird lay. She matted it together and spread it over the bird, to provide some warmth in the cold earth.

"Good-bye, dear bird," she said. "Good-bye, and thank you for your lovely song this summer, when all the trees were green and the sun shone so warmly on us." Then she laid her head against the bird's breast. But suddenly she started, for something seemed to be pounding deep inside. It was the bird's heart. The bird was not dead; he lay in a deep daze, and now that he was being warmed he was coming to life again.

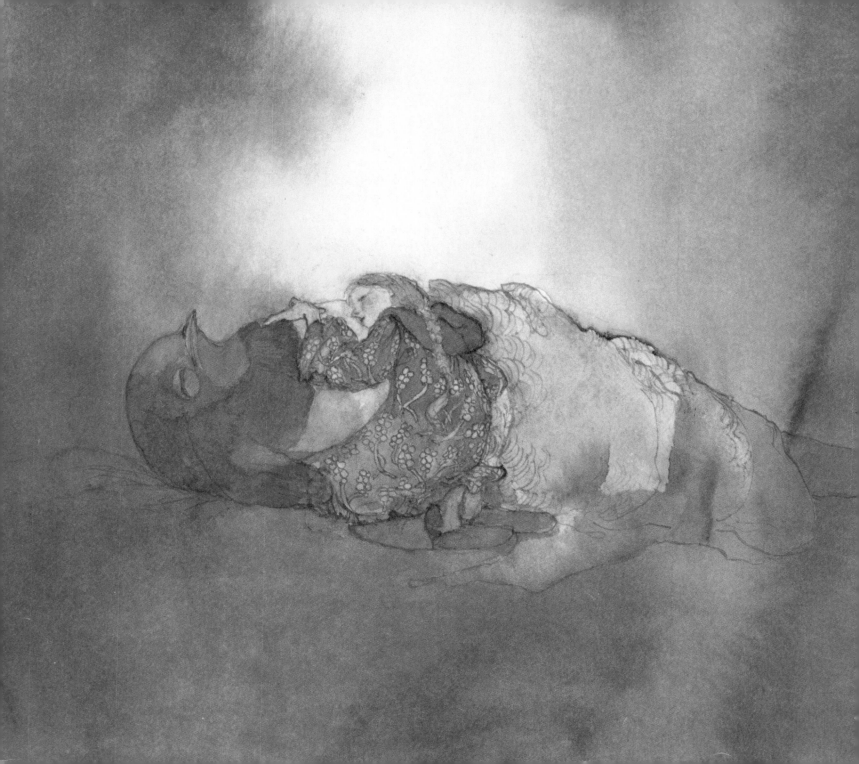

"Thank you very much, dear little girl," the sick swallow said to her. "I am nicely warmed up now. Soon I will get my strength back and be able to fly again, out into the warm sunshine."

"Oh," she said, "it is cold outside, snowing and blowing. Stay in your warm bed, and I will take care of you."

She brought the swallow water in a flower petal, and he drank and told her how he had hurt one of his wings on a briar bush and so could not keep up with the other swallows when they set off for the warm country. At last he had dropped to the ground, but he could not remember any more and did not know how he had come here.

All winter long the swallow stayed in the tunnel, and Thumbeline took care of him lovingly. But she never let either the mole or the field mouse know what she was doing, for they had only dislike for the poor bird.

As soon as spring came and the sun's warmth could be felt even underground, the swallow said good-bye to Thumbeline. She opened up the hole in the ceiling, which the mole had covered over. The sun shone in deliciously, and the swallow asked whether she did not want to come with him. She could sit on his back; they would fly out into the greenwood together. But Thumbeline knew that it would grieve the old field mouse if she left her.

"No, I cannot," Thumbeline said.

"Good-bye, good-bye, you good, lovely girl!" the swallow said, and flew off into the sunshine. Thumbeline watched him, and her eyes filled with tears, for she was so fond of the poor swallow.

"Kee-wit, kee-wit," the bird sang, as he flew into the greenwood.

Thumbeline's heart was heavy. She was not allowed to go out into the warm sunshine. The field above the field mouse's house had been sown with grain; the stalks were already tall, making a dense woods for the little girl who was no bigger than a thumb.

"Now that it's summer you must prepare for your wedding," the field mouse said to her, for the neighbor, the boring old mole in his black-velvet coat, had made his marriage proposal. "I want you to be well outfitted with both woolens and linens. Once you are the mole's wife, you will have all the comforts."

Thumbeline had to spend long hours at spinning, and the field mouse also hired four spiders to spin and weave for her day and night. Every evening the mole came to see them and was always talking about how the summer would be over soon. For at the moment the sun was so hot that the earth was being baked almost as hard as stone. Yes, when summer was over his wedding with Thumbeline would take place. But she was not at all pleased by this kind of talk, for she did not care at all for the boring mole. Every morning, when the sun rose, and every evening when it set, she slipped out the door, and when the wind parted the barley stems so that she could see the blue sky she thought of how bright and beautiful it was out there and wished that she could catch sight of the dear swallow again. But the swallow never came back; surely he was flying far away in the lovely green woods.

By the time fall came, all the spinning and weaving was done.

"You will have your wedding in four weeks!" the field mouse said to Thumbeline. But Thumbeline wept and said she did not want to marry the boring mole.

"Stuff and nonsense," the field mouse said. "Don't be stubborn or you'll feel how sharp my teeth are. He's a well set-up gentleman, he is, and the queen herself has nothing finer than his black-velvet coat. His kitchens and cellars are crammed full. You ought to be very thankful for him."

So the time for the wedding came around. The mole was already there to take Thumbeline away; she was to live with him deep down underground, never come out into the warm sunlight, which he could not tolerate. The poor child was heartbroken, for she must say farewell to the sunlight, which up to now, in the field mouse's house, she had at least seen now and then from the doorway.

"Good-bye, bright sun," she said, stretching her arms high into the air. She went a little way off from the field mouse's house, for once again the grain had been cut and only the short dry stubble remained. "Good-bye, good-bye!" she said, throwing her arms around a little red flower that stood there. "Greet the dear swallow if you chance to see him."

"Kee-wit, kee-wit," came from overhead at that very moment. She looked up. It was the swallow, just flying by. The moment he caught sight of Thumbeline he stopped in delight. She told her old friend how she was supposed to take the ugly mole for her husband and that she would have to live deep underground, where the sun never shone. As she spoke to him, she could not stop crying.

"Now the cold winter is coming," the swallow said. "I am flying far away to the warm country. Will you come with me? You can ride on my back. Tie yourself tightly with your sash, and we will fly far from the ugly mole and his dark house, over the mountains to the warm country where the sun shines brighter than here, for it is always summer there and flowers bloom all year round. Do fly with me, sweet little Thumbeline, who saved my life when I lay frozen in the dark tunnel."

"Yes, I will go with you," Thumbeline said, and she mounted the bird's back, with her feet resting on his outspread wings. She tied her sash tightly to one of the strongest feathers, and off the swallow flew, high into the air, over forest and over sea, high above the tall mountains forever capped with snow. Thumbeline shivered in the cold air, but then she snuggled down under the bird's warm feathers, only raising her little head to see all the beauty beneath her.

So they came to the warm country. There the sun shone more brightly than she had ever seen it. The sky was twice as high there, and green and purple grapes grew on the terraced hillsides. Lemons and oranges hung in the groves; the air was fragrant with myrtle and mint, and beautiful children ran about playing with big, multicolored butterflies. Yet still the swallow flew on and on, and everything became lovelier and lovelier. Under the tall, green trees by a blue lake gleamed a white marble castle from olden times. Vines twisted around the tall pillars. On the tallest pillar were many swallows' nests, and in one of them lived the swallow that was carrying Thumbeline.

"This is my house," the swallow said. "But if you want to find one for yourself, choose one of the finest flowers that grows below. I'll set you down there, and you will find it the most blessed place imaginable to live."

"That would be nice," Thumbeline said, and clapped her small hands.

There lay a great white marble pillar that had fallen to the ground and broken into three pieces; between these pieces grew the most beautiful big white flowers she had ever seen. The swallow flew down with Thumbeline and set her on the wide petals. But how astonished she was, for there sat a little man in the middle of the flower, as clear and transparent as if he were made of glass. He had a finely wrought golden crown on his head and lovely transparent wings on his shoulders. The little man was no bigger than Thumbeline. He was the spirit of the flower. Down there, a little man or woman lived in every flower, but this one was king of all the rest.

"Goodness, how handsome he is," Thumbeline whispered to the swallow. The little prince was frightened by the swallow, for the bird was gigantic compared to him who was so small and delicate. But when he caught sight of Thumbeline, his joy was very great, for she was the most beautiful girl he had ever seen. So he took his golden crown from his head, placed it on hers, asked her name and whether she would be his wife. If so, she would become queen of all the flowers. Yes, here was a proper sort of husband, different from a toad's son or a mole with a black-velvet coat. So she said Yes to the handsome prince, and from every flower stepped out a lady or a gentleman, each more charming than the last, so that it was a delight to see them. Each brought Thumbeline a present, but the best of all was a pair of fine wings. They were fastened to Thumbeline's back, and now she too could fly from flower to flower. What a delight that was! The swallow perched on his nest and sang for them as well as he could, but there was sorrow in his heart, for he was fond of Thumbeline and never wanted to be parted from her.

"You should not be called Thumbeline," the spirit of the flowers said to her. "That is an ugly name, and you are so beautiful. We will call you Maya."

"Good-bye, good-bye," the swallow called, and flew away again from the warm country, far, far back to Denmark. There he had a little nest over the window of the man who likes to write books for children. The swallow sang to him, "Kee-wit, kee-wit," and he wrote it down. So that is how we come to know this whole story.